SONG IN THE CITY

Words by
Daniel Bernstrom

Pictures by
Jenin Mohammed

HARPER
An Imprint of HarperCollinsPublishers

Sunday morning, Emmalene heard a sing-along song,
a busy city symphony that followed her along!

TAP-TAPPA-TAP
YIP-YIPPA-YIP
SIZZLE-SIZZLE
HONKY-HONK
Pitter-patter—

Running for the bus, by the busy-busy street,

a (((CHONK!)))

then a SCREECH!

then a

BEEP, BEEP, **BEEP**!

"Grandma Jean!" said Emmalene.
"Did you hear that pretty ditty?"
"Emmalene," said Grandma Jean.
"Cross the street while it's not busy."

"What you're hearing is commotion.
Oh, my child, what a notion!
That is traffic you are hearing, not a song."

BOOM came the bus.

Two doors KA-CLUNKED wide.

The driver mumbled,

Come inside.

Tickets

BEE-BEEPED!

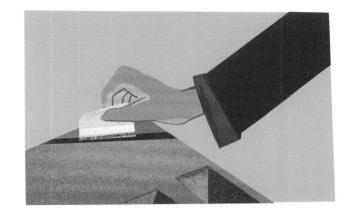

Shoes

CLICKITY-CLOMPED.

RUMBLE

went the engine in a rollicking romp.

"Grandma Jean!" said Emmalene.
"Do you hear that drumming beat?"

"Emmalene!" said Grandma Jean.
"We are moving! Take a seat!"

Then, all of a sudden, they came to a stop.
Outside of the window marched a

"Grandma Jean!" said Emmalene.
"Don't you hear that tinkling tune?"

"*Emmalene,*" said Grandma Jean,
"*we'll be getting off here soon.*"

"Grandma, listen to the city!"

"Don't you see right now I'm busy?
I have told you, that's the city, not a song."

Outside of the church,

wind **FLAPPED** bright clothes.

Wind **SPRINKLED** rain.

Wind **SCATTERED** crows.

Wind **rattled** branches.

Wind **CRINKLED** leaves.

Wind
RAINED
down acorns from oak trees.

Wind
DRUMMED
the world with a
tippity-tapping...

In the church, in the pew,
Grandma clapped as trumpets blew.
And the choir raised a chorus
with a music loud and joyous.

"*Emmalene,*" sang Grandma Jean,
"*now, I tell you, that's a song.*"

"Just forget it, Grandma Jean.
What I say just comes out wrong."

Emmalene left Grandma Jean,
and she vanished out the back.
Grandma Jean sat all alone,
holding tight her Sunday hat.

Grandma Jean found Emmalene.
"What on earth is going on?"

"Grandma Jean," said Emmalene,
"you're not getting what I mean."

"Can't you hear that backhoe

drumming

or the city sirens

humming?

Do you hear the

clap-clap-clapping

of the pitter-patting rain?

Or the

toot-tooting

whistle of the passing cargo train?

Do you hear the choir
singing
with the
ringing
of the city?"

"Grandma Jean—I mean—really!
You're not trying and it's silly.
If you'd only stop and listen, there's a song!"

"Do you really hear a song?" asked Grandma Jean.
"It's playing now," said Emmalene.

"Then sit with me," said Grandma Jean,
"and I'll listen to the city.
Frankly, child, I've been busy,
but I'll listen to the city for your song."

She sat stock-still,
tried not to yawn.
She listened as the world played on.
But what she heard was nothing new.

Some people sang.

Some trumpets blew.

She heard the wind,
a few crass crows,

a crying cat,
some crinkling clothes,

a train . . . somewhere?

A bus BEEP-BEEPED!

A cell phone BUZZED.

A siren SHRIEKED.

Then one hand darkened Grandma Jean's eyes.
"Try this way."

And Grandma Jean tried.

Acorns

ticked.

A backhoe

WRecKeD

A truck

HARRUMPH'ED

And birds

Peck-
pecked.

Then all at once the noise went still.
Did she hear a dancing drill?
A far-off siren in a soulful serenade?

Then wait . . .
What was that music being played?

The song and city filled Grandma Jean's ears.

She hugged Emmalene.
She fought back tears.
"Grandma Jean?" asked Emmalene.
"Is something wrong?"

"No, no," she cried.
"I hear your song."

Then they listened to the city,
to the CLAPPING
FLAPPING
tippity-tapping
BIPPITY-BOPPING
rollicky-romping
CLICKITY-CLOMPING
BEEPING–YIPPING music of the city.

They listened to the city and the song.

To Minnesota State Services for the Blind and to Dr. Barkmeier
and the Mayo Clinic. Thank you for taking time to listen.
—D.B.

To Mommy, my very first teacher.
Thank you for inspiring my love of
illustration and mixed media.
—J.M.

Library of Congress Control Number: 2021941319
ISBN 978-0-06-301112-0

The artist used Photoshop to create the digital illustrations for this book.
Typography by Rachel Zegar
22 23 24 25 26 RTLO 10 9 8 7 6 5 4 3 2 1 ❖ First Edition